A First Word Bank

Ruth Thomson

Chrysalis Children's Books

First published in the UK in 2002 by
Chrysalis Children's Books
An imprint of Chrysalis Books Group Plc
The Chrysalis Building, Bramley Road,
London W10 6SP

Paperback edition first published in 2004

ISBN 1-84138-264-7 (hb)
ISBN 1-84138-852-1 (pb)
British Library Cataloguing in Publication Data
for this book is available from the British Library.

Editor: Mary-Jane Wilkins
Designers: Rachel Hamdi, Holly Mann
Illustrators: Patrice Aggs, Becky Blake,
Louise Comfort, Charlotte Hard, Brenda Haw,
Jan McAfferty, Kevin McAleenan, Kevin Maddison,
Holly Mann, Melanie Mansfield, Colin Payne,
Lisa Smith, Sara Walker, Gwyneth Williamson
Educational consultant: Pie Corbett, Poet and
Consultant to the National Literacy Strategy

Printed in Hong Kong
10 9 8 7 6 5 4 3 2 1 (hb)
10 9 8 7 6 5 4 3 2 1 (pb)

Contents

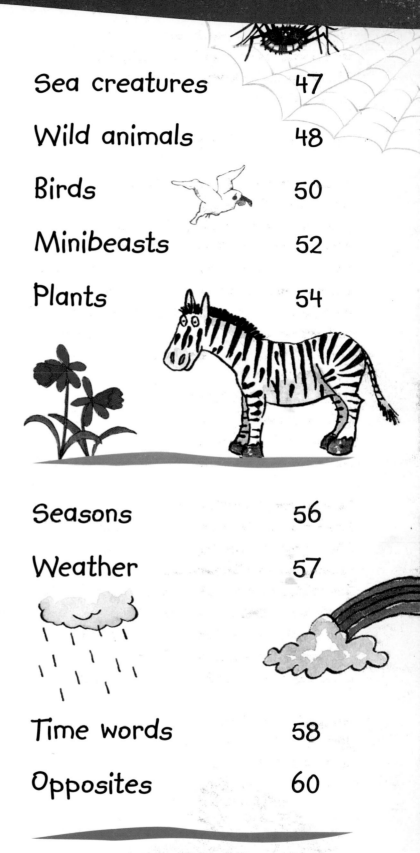

About this book

This word bank is a resource of carefully chosen words to help young children develop their vocabulary.

How to use this book

Every spread can be used for discussion, for playing word games, to provide words for writing and as a spell-check.

The illustrated words are divided into categories. Some are labelled as examples for children to follow. A useful word box lists adjectives, verbs or extra nouns.

Children can also think up their own words and sentences. Try brainstorming ideas on a theme before children start to write.

theme heading

category heading

labelled illustration

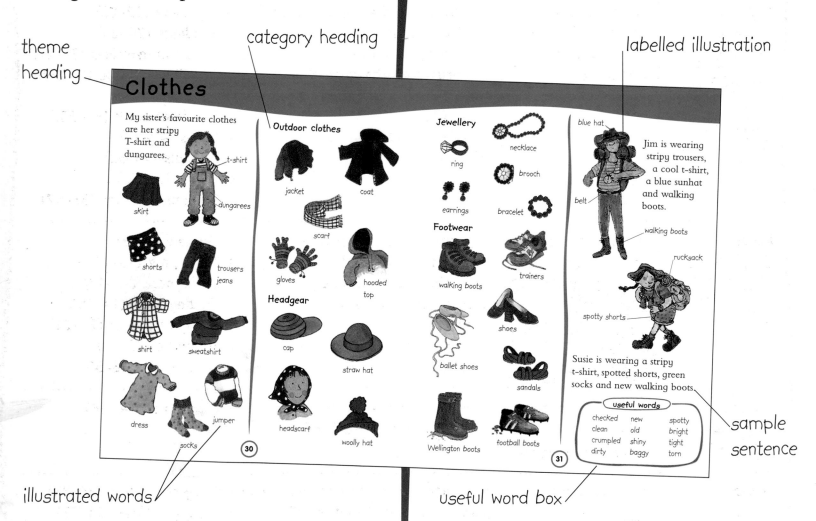

illustrated words

useful word box

sample sentence

The words are arranged by theme and also by type of writing. Each spread gives a choice of words on a theme and a sentence which shows some of the words in use.

Types of writing

Writing has many different purposes, language features and forms. The types of writing that children initially learn are laid out in the chart opposite.

Text type	Purpose	Features	Word bank themes
Labels	✧ Identification	✧ Often written as single words ✧ Usually nouns ✧ Sometimes used with lines or arrows connected to the the picture	✧ Parts of a bicycle (16) ✧ Parts of a spaceship (17) ✧ School equipment (18–19) ✧ Machines (27) ✧ Parts of the body (28) ✧ Parts of a cat (44) ✧ Parts of a bird (50) ✧ Parts of an insect (52) ✧ Parts of a plant (54)
Lists	✧ Reminders ✧ Planning	✧ Written in note form ✧ Each item written on a separate line	✧ Going shopping (40–41)
Reports	✧ To describe things or people: their qualities, behaviour, habits or uses	✧ Written in the present tense, eg Trees are plants. ✧ Non-chronological ✧ Focuses on the general rather than an individual, eg Doctors look after ill people. Not Dr Parks looks after Sam.	✧ My home (22–23) ✧ Buildings (24–25) ✧ Tools and machines (26–27) ✧ Describing people (28–29) ✧ Clothes (30–31) ✧ People at work (32–33) ✧ Meals (42–43) ✧ Animals (44–53) ✧ Plants (54–55) ✧ Seasons/Weather (56–57)
Recounts	✧ To retell events	✧ Written in the past tense, eg I went to the park. ✧ In chronological order, ie first, next, after, last. ✧ Focus on a particular person or people, eg I, he, she, we, they, Jim.	✧ My news (8–9) ✧ Party time (10–11) ✧ In the park (12–13) ✧ Holiday time (14–15) ✧ A day at school (20–21) ✧ My home (22–23) ✧ Time words (58–59)
Explanation	✧ To explain how things work or why something happens	✧ Written in the present tense, eg You push the pedals of a bike.	✧ Ways to travel (16)
Stories	✧ To entertain	✧ Written in the first or third person (I, he, she) and usually written in the past tense ✧ Chronological ✧ About human or animal characters – good and bad ✧ May include dialogue ✧ Use adjectives and powerful verbs	✧ Story characters (34–35) ✧ Story creatures (36–37) ✧ Story objects (38–39) Useful words also appear in: ✧ My dream factory (27) ✧ Describing people (28–29) ✧ Clothes (30–31) ✧ Weather (57) ✧ Time words (58–59)

Doctors look after people who are hurt or ill. Some work in hospitals. They treat people and give them medicines to help make them better.

At the weekend Dad took us to a theme park. First we swung on the swingboats. Then we rode on the roller coaster. After that we queued for a turn on the big wheel.

One day she met a friendly dragon.

Word games

You can use the themed spreads to play all sorts of word games. These will help children expand their vocabulary, develop their reading skills and improve their memory and concentration.

I went to market

Play this old favourite with the Shopping spread *(p40–41)*. The first player says:

I went to market and bought some apples.

The next player repeats the sentence, adding a new item:

I went to market and bought some apples and some cheese…

Change the game by asking players to add an adjective to their word, such as its colour or shape. Players can also choose a food item in alphabetical order, eg apples, bananas, carrots, etc.

Vary the game by changing the place or situation, eg:

I went on holiday and took…*(p14)*

I went to a café and ordered…*(p42)*

I went to the toy shop and bought…*(p11)*

I opened the treasure chest and found… *(p38)*

What is it?

Take turns to describe three features of a wild animal using the pictures *(p48–49)* to help you, eg:

This animal is brown, shaggy and has horns.

You could also say which letter sound the animal's name begins with, eg:

This hairy animal begins with y *(yak)*.

You could add extra information, eg:

This black and white animal is very smelly.

Dressing up

Take turns to dress a person, using the clothes pictures (p30–31). Each player chooses a person and a garment, plus an adjective that begins with the same letter, saying eg:

> I will dress a boy
> in shiny shorts.
> or
> I will dress a fine lady
> in a crooked crown.
> or
> I will dress a girl
> in dirty dungarees.

They can go on to invent some other outfits, eg:

> a beautiful ballgown or clumping clogs

What's my job?

One player chooses one of the people at work (p32–33), but doesn't tell the other players which one it is. The other players ask questions in turn to find out which person it is, eg:

Do you work outside?	Yes
Do you help build houses?	No
Do you keep the streets clean?	Yes
Are you a road sweeper?	Yes

You could also play this game with story characters (p34).

Making sentences

Open the book at any theme. Take turns to choose two words on that theme and ask the other players to make up as many sentences as they can using both words, eg: mouse, bone:

> The mouse found a bone.
>
> The mouse hid behind a bone.
>
> A bone is bigger than a mouse.

When no one can think of any more, choose another pair of words.

Mystery objects

Take turns to think of an object. Say what it is, eg:

> It is a vegetable.

Describe what it looks like, eg:

> It is long, hard and orange.

Say where it is found (or what it is used for), eg:

> It grows underground.
>
> It can be eaten raw or cooked.

Can other players guess what it is? Use pictures of home (p22–23), tools (p26), clothes (p30) and story objects (p38).

My news

Places

On Saturday afternoon Mum and Dad took us to the cinema. After that, I stayed the night at Sam's and we played with his kitten. On Sunday we went for a bike ride.

cinema
film

country

park

market

friend's house

granny's house

café

museum

show

castle

carnival

Activities

rode my bike

watched TV
watched a video

made a den

flew my kite

played snakes
and ladders

washed the dog

played with the dog

practised
the recorder

went rowing

played baseball

went shopping

did a jigsaw
puzzle

drew some pictures

useful words		
sister	cousin	visited
brother	uncle	saw
gran	aunt	watched
friend	grandad	drove

Party time

rabbit   spaceman   cat   pirate   King   flower   cowboy

Fancy-dress party

On Saturday, I went to
Jamie's fancy-dress party.
Joe dressed up as a pirate
and I went as a cat.
A clown did funny tricks
and we played hide-and-seek.

fairy

princess and
prince

popstars

Party things

sweets

streamers

magician
conjuror
entertainer

balloons

invitation

birthday cake

birthday cards

clown

Presents

bike

ball

kite

glider

gloves

camera

fish tank

skates

yo-yo

car

sketchbook

robot

book

scarf

goggles

kitten

crayons

recorder

game

bracelet

globe

jeep

teddy

soft toy

CD

piggy bank

11

jigsaw puzzle

fort

In the park

Yesterday we met some friends in the park for a game of frisbee.

frisbee

grass

birds

boat

fountain

football

swing

path

slide

gardener

scooter

bridge

climbing frame

sandpit

tree

ducks

flowerbed

picnic

useful words

played	climbed	found
kicked	ran	walked
fed	watched	slid
threw	hid	rode

At the weekend Dad took us to a theme park. First we swung on the swingboats. Then we rode on the roller coaster. After that we queued for a turn on the big wheel.

big wheel

roller coaster

carousel

water splash

dodgems

ghost train

simulator

swingboats

roundabout

entrance

queue

toffee

helter skelter

crowd

lollipop

candyfloss

useful words

crashed	twisted	glided
smashed	plunged	whirred
splashed	rolled	rocked
spun	whirled	zoomed

Holiday time

Places to go

In the summer holidays we went to stay at the seaside. We played on the beach every day.

seaside

town
city

mountains

river

country

Things to take on holiday

T-shirt

camera

suitcase

backpack

sun cream

swimsuit

torch

skis

sandals

flippers

bat

ball

map

goggles

frisbee

towel

rug

tent

At the seaside

gull

One day we built an enormous sandcastle and decorated it with stones and shells. After that we buried Dad in the sand.

shells

sandcastle

bucket

cliffs

surfer

surfboard

rocks

crab

fishing boat   waves   sea

In the country

butterfly

farm

bees

tractor

field

hive

birds

cockerel

sheep

flowers

hill

forest
wood

fence

useful words

dug	climbed	explored
paddled	collected	made
swam	walked	pretended
threw	watched	met

Ways to travel

Parts of a bicycle

saddle

brake

reflector

mudguard

handlebars

pump

back wheel

tyre

chain

pedal

spokes

You push the pedals of a bike to make the wheels turn. The faster you pedal, the faster the bike goes.

On land

tricycle

racing car

motorbike

lorry
truck

car

van

train

bus

tractor

16

useful words		
key	seat belt	steering wheel
start	brake	gear lever
stop	petrol	windscreen
engine	helmet	accelerator

On water

rowing boat

tug

trawler
fishing boat

yacht
sailing boat

liner
ship

speedboat

In the air

aeroplane
jet

helicopter

glider

hot-air balloon

In space

To take off into space you climb up the ramp into the rocket. You strap yourself in and press the buttons to start the countdown. Then you blast off.

rocket

Parts of a spaceship

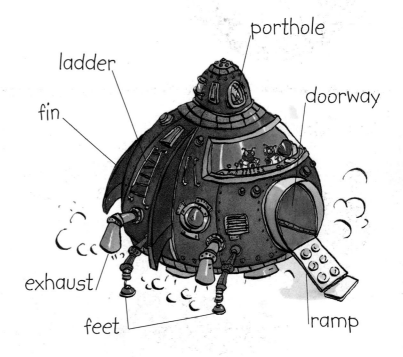

porthole

ladder

fin

doorway

exhaust

feet

ramp

useful words

zoom	skim	lift off
land	sail	soar
speed	flash	roar
whirr	hurtle	whizz

We made labels for everything in our classroom.

globe

puppets

bricks

clock

pencil sharpeners

scissors

rulers

crayons

pencils

pens

string

glue

coat hooks

trays

shelves

books

chairs

cushions

cuddly toy

18

aquarium
fish food
paintbrushes
pictures
paints
paper towels
modelling clay
model
plant
easel
taps
scissors
scraper
roller
sink
paper

map
photographs
markers

$$6 + 10 = 16$$
$$10 + 10 = 20$$

whiteboard
screen
paper
printer
computer
mouse
keyboard

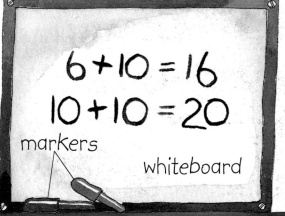

useful words

writing area	reading folders
art area	drawing paper
worksheets	coloured paper
writing paper	computer corner
felt-tips	trolley

A day at school

Today we are making paper butterflies. We are cutting them from shiny paper.

dancing

imagining

counting

reading

measuring

weighing

sorting

writing

comparing

planting

painting

sticki...

making

drawing

looking at

colouring

playing

Yesterday we talked about insects.

sang

pretended

clapped

watched

useful words

compared	cut	read
painted	counted	made
measured	wrote	drew
looked at	played	stuck

My home

Where do you live?
I live in a flat on the third floor.

flats

house

Living room

sofa

mirror

fish tank

armchair

vase

telephone

lamp

television

What is your bedroom like?
I share a bedroom with my brother. We have bunk beds and loads of toys.

bunk beds

toy basket

radio ghettoblaster

blanket

pillow

Bathroom

soap

sponge

toothpaste

toothbrush

soap dish

taps

towel

bath

Kitchen

fridge

clock

stool

table

high chair

tray

broom

Utensils

cheese grater

whisk

knife

chopping board

tea towel

wooden spoon

saucepan

jug

fork

frying pan

sieve

colander

scales

mixing bowl

Crockery

dishes

teapot

saucers

cups

sugar bowl

bowl

dinner plates

side plates

serving plate

gravy boat

Buildings

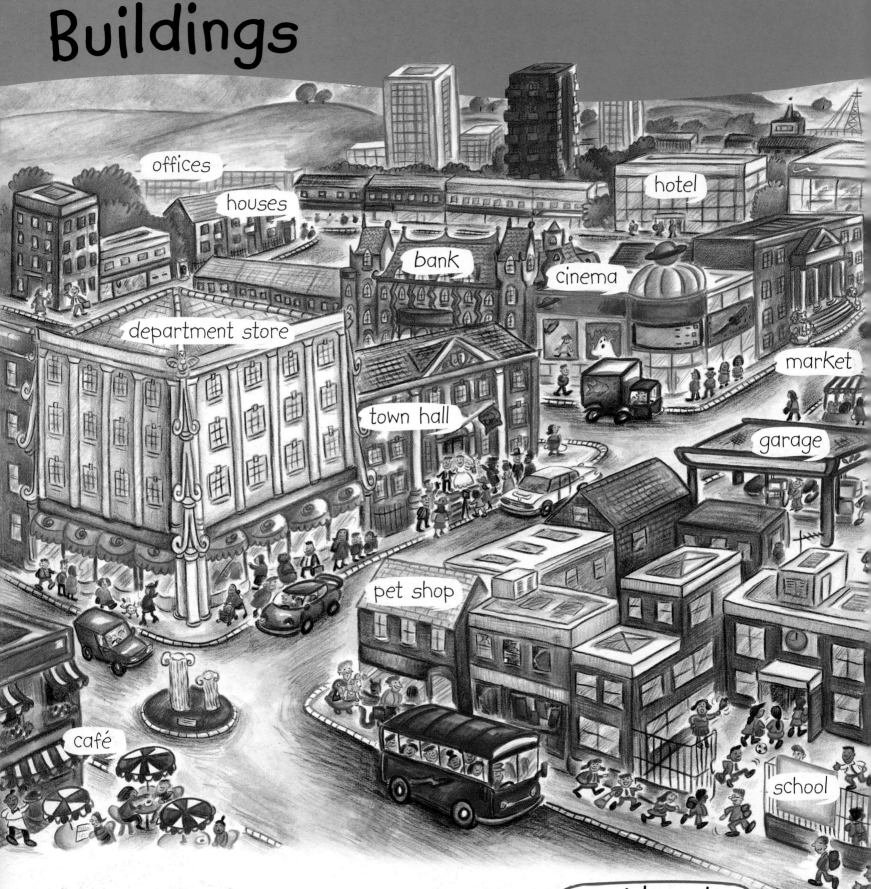

At the garage you can buy petrol.
You can watch films at the cinema.
At the market you can buy fruit
and vegetables.

useful words

work	learn	make things
worship	stay	get married
eat	drink	get better
get money	swim	play football

chi...
fl...
hospital
museum
flats
shops
funnel
gauge
toffee
lemon
gooey
nutty

leisure centre
swimming pool
school
church
skyscrapers
fire station
mosque
factory
supermarket
house

Describing people

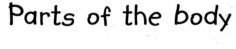

pliers

scre

spann

Paint

paint

Parts of the body

eye

eyebrow

nose

ear

cheek

mouth

thumb

arm

elbow

palm

hand

finger

leg

foot

toe

knee

Hair

curly

long

bunches

short

dark

fair

What people look like

old

fat
plump
rounded

young

strong
muscly

thin
skinny

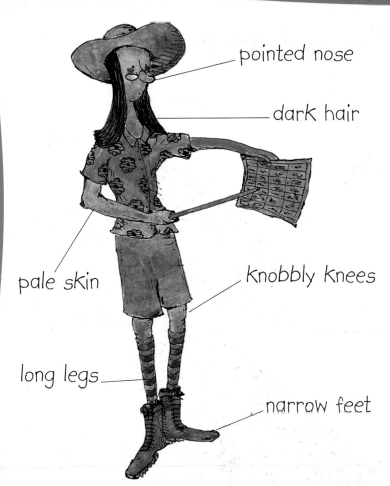

pointed nose

dark hair

pale skin

knobbly knees

long legs

narrow feet

Jane is tall and has dark hair.

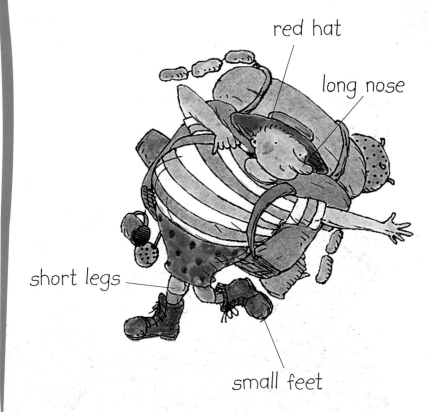

red hat

long nose

short legs

small feet

(29)

Ben is short and has
a long nose.

Clothes

My sister's favourite clothes are her stripy T-shirt and dungarees.

skirt

T-shirt

dungarees

shorts

trousers
jeans

shirt

sweatshirt

dress

socks

jumper

Outdoor clothes

jacket

coat

scarf

gloves

hooded
top

Headgear

cap

straw hat

headscarf

woolly hat

30

Jewellery

necklace

ring

brooch

bracelet

earrings

Footwear

walking boots

trainers

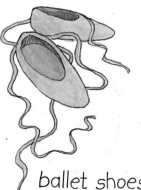
ballet shoes

shoes

sandals

Wellington boots

football boots

blue sunhat

Jim is wearing stripy trousers, a cool T-shirt, a blue sunhat and walking boots.

belt

stripy trousers

walking boots

stripy T-shirt

spotted shorts

new boots

Susie is wearing a stripy T-shirt, spotted shorts, green socks and new walking boots.

useful words

check	warm	smart
clean	old	bright
crumpled	shiny	tight
creased	baggy	torn

People at work

builder

dustman

bus driver

pilot

bricklayer

plumber

lorry driver

mechanic

window cleaner

road sweeper

racing driver

messenger

writer

photographer

TV cameraperson

computer operator

10 + 4 =
20 + 4 =
30 + 4 =

teacher

newsreader

supermarket
worker

waiter

ballet dancer

shopkeeper

baseball player

footballer

gardener

vet

farmer

hairdresser

dentist

optician

nurse

doctor

Doctors look after people
who are hurt or ill.
Some work in hospitals.
They treat people
and give them medicines
to help make them better.

(33)

Story characters

witch

thief

> Once upon a time, there was a lonely princess.

People

queen

prince

princess

sailor

shepherd

soldier

family

king

pirate

giant

old man and old woman

farmer

mermaid

Goldilocks

emperor

elf

clown

Knight

She lived on her own in a palace tower.

palace

fort

cottage

tower

castle

village

useful words

beautiful	sad	rich
charming	poor	silly
cruel	powerful	wicked
happy	pretty	young

Story creatures

One day she met
a friendly dragon.

bear

lion

dragon

cat

hen

monkey

mouse

dinosaur

gingerbread
man

alien

troll

crocodile

toad

goats

fox

frog

fairy

monster

pig

horse

genie

wolf

Story settings

He took her for a walk in the dark forest.

forest

swamp

lake

mountains

cave

desert

useful words

crafty	hairy	timid
enormous	huge	tiny
fierce	proud	ugly
gentle	silent	wise

37

Story objects

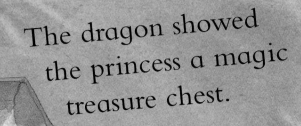

The dragon showed the princess a magic treasure chest.

sword

rope

invitation

treasure chest

goblet

veil

basket

mirror

crown

present

fire

ring

key

glass slipper

wand

coins

throne

mask

spell book

38

turban

witch's hat

When the princess opened the lid, smoke billowed out, hiding everything from view...

well

telescope

smoke

flying carpet

coach and horses

fountain

feast

spaceship

boat

clock

ship

moon

island

army cavalcade

useful words

shiny	rusty	splendid
glittering	gorgeous	golden
sparkling	heavy	great
mysterious	dazzling	delicate

Going shopping

I helped Mum write our shopping list for the weekend. Then we went to town to buy all the food.

Shopping list

Two cartons of milk
A dozen eggs
A loaf of bread
A packet of sausages
A pack of butter
1 kg apples
A bunch of bananas

Groceries

eggs

jam

rice

cheese

yogurt

milk

chocolate

butter

tomato ketchup

biscuits
cookies

bread

spaghetti

Meat and fish

burgers

ham

chicken

fish fingers

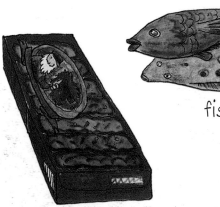
fish

sausages

Vegetables

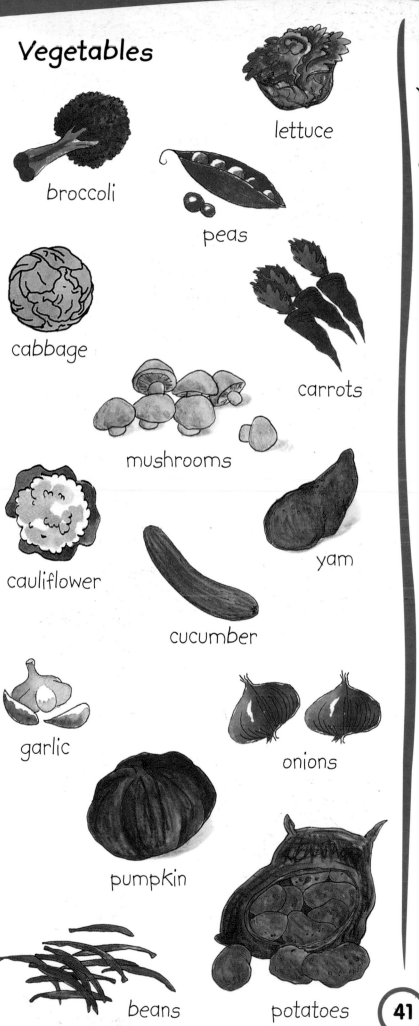

broccoli

lettuce

peas

cabbage

carrots

mushrooms

cauliflower

cucumber

yam

garlic

onions

pumpkin

beans

potatoes

Fruit

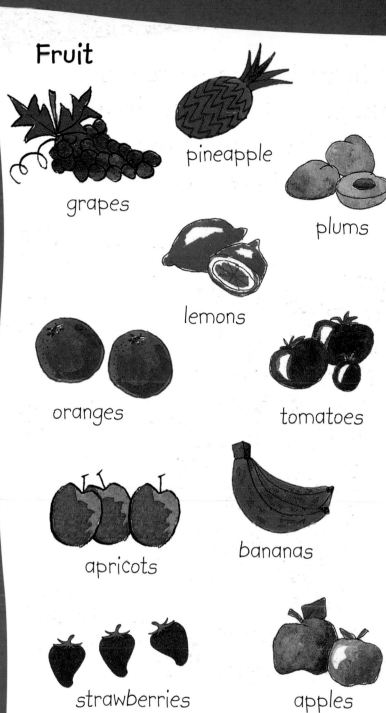

grapes

pineapple

plums

lemons

oranges

tomatoes

apricots

bananas

strawberries

apples

cherries

useful words

jar	bunch	bottle
box	pack	bag
packet	bar	basket
tin	slab	kilo

Meals

I have a bowl
of cereal, a glass
of orange juice and
some toast for breakfast.

jam

orange juice

toast

cereal

bread

drinking chocolate

Snacks

cake

muffin

sandwich

biscuits

nuts

crisps

apple

fruit

fruit cake

useful words

cup	piece	bag
mug	spoonful	warm
plate	handful	cold
carton	slice	chilled

My favourite food is chocolate
cake. I like it because
it is sweet and sticky.

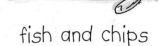
fish and chips

chocolate cake

apple pie

salad

pancakes

baked potato

burger and chips

stew

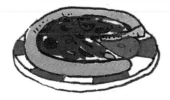
pizza

soup

chips

spaghetti
bolognese

chicken leg

omelette

fruit salad

bread and cheese

ice cream

43

useful words		
creamy	crunchy	smooth
chewy	gooey	spicy
crisp	juicy	hot
crumbly	mushy	tangy

Pets

My pet

dog

spider

puppies

snake

hamster

mouse

rabbit

parrot

goldfish

cat and kitten

(44)

Parts of a cat

ears

eyes

nose

whiskers

fur

collar

tail

paws

I have a pet cat.
His name is Tom.
He has a soft black coat.
He is bouncy and friendly.

useful words

noisy	hairy	nosy
clean	dirty	playful
clever	scaly	furry
cuddly	quiet	lazy

Where pets sleep

Tom sleeps on my bed.

armchair

bird cage

fish tank

basket

hutch

jar

What pets eat

Tom eats pet food.

cheese

pet food

lettuce

bird seed

bones

fish

What pets do

When I stroke him,
Tom purrs.

run

hide

sleep

play

splash

scratch

(45)

useful words

barks	howls	squeaks
growls	screeches	yaps
hisses	snarls	yelps
miaows	snuffles	yowls

Farm animals

Hens lay eggs. They sit on the eggs to keep them warm. Chicks hatch from the eggs. Chicks are baby hens.

chicks

hen

cockerel

bull

cow   calf

pig   piglet

duck   duckling

sheep   lamb

horse   foal

bees
beehive

goat

kid

goose

turkey

donkey

useful words

sty	stable	gosling
field	barn	larva
pen	pond	scratch
nest	hen house	peck

Sea creatures

Dolphins swim around in families.
They talk to each other with
clicking and squeaking noises.

dolphins

turtle

whale

starfish

angelfish

shark

seahorse

seal

crab

oysters

lobster

electric eel

jellyfish

coral

useful words

fins	tail	claws
scales	rocks	seabed
glide	cling	dive
float	grow	hide

Wild animals

An elephant is **enormous**.
It has a long trunk
and sharp tusks.

elephant

monkey

anteater

tortoise

leopard

cheetah

camel

sloth

zebra

orang-utan

yak

bear and cub

platypus

reindeer

baboon

kangaroo

48

lizard

crocodile

koala

skunk

beaver

tiger

panda

lion

giraffe

hare

otter

snake

antelope

deer

fox

wolf

(49)

useful words		
furry	massive	rough
tiny	playful	speedy
fierce	sleek	strong
smelly	hairy	huge

Birds

Parts of a bird

beak

eye

feathers

wing

claws
talons

tail

Owls are birds of prey.
They have large round eyes.
They sleep during the day
and fly at night.

swallow

seagull

flamingo

peacock

eagle

hawk

parrot

vulture

ostrich

goose

swan

stork

Where birds live

Owls live in farm buildings, hollow trees or caves.

towns

cliffs

fields

mountains

caves

woods
trees

marsh

river

Owls lay eggs. They make a nest for the eggs. The eggs hatch into chicks.

Bird food

Owls hunt at night for small animals, such as mice.

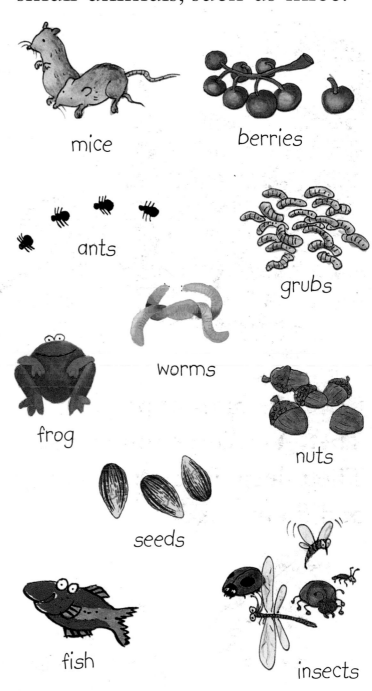

mice

berries

ants

grubs

worms

frog

nuts

seeds

fish

insects

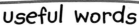

useful words		
build	hover	perch
catch	roost	search
flap	dive	soar
glide	peck	swoop

Minibeasts

Parts of an insect

All insects have a head, a thorax, an abdomen and six legs. Some have wings.

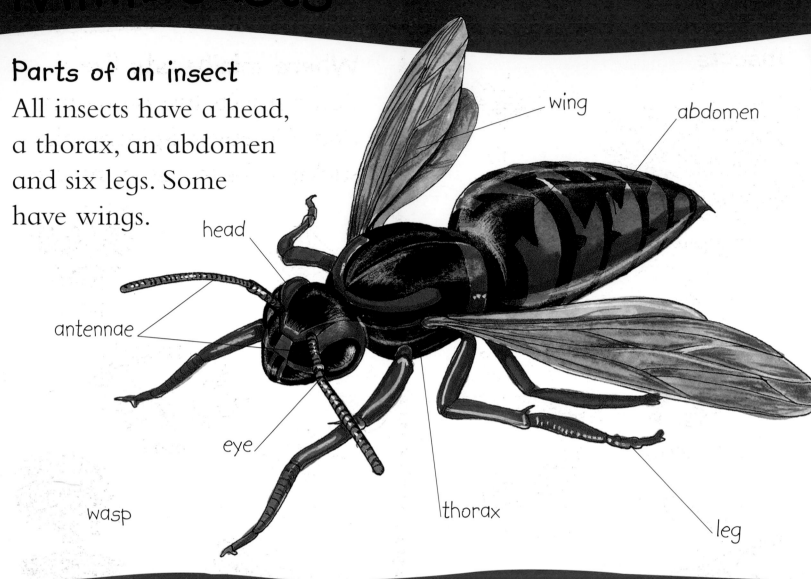

wing

abdomen

head

antennae

eye

wasp

thorax

leg

Creepy-crawlies

Some creepy-crawlies have lots of legs. Slugs and snails have no legs at all.

slug

spider

snail

worm

woodlouse

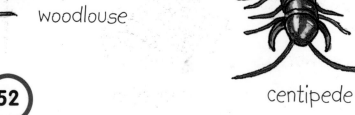

centipede

Parts o...

Th...
Lig...
the...
lik...
spl...

leaves

trunk

bark

leaf

tree stum...

Insects

mosquitoes

fly

butterfly

beetles

caterpillar

dragonfly

grasshopper

ants

bee

glow-worm

ladybird

Where minibeasts live

Some insects live on plants
and eat leaves. Spiders spin
sticky webs to catch insects.

web

plant

pond

nettles

flowers

tree

wall

grass

useful words

burrow	grow	lay
crawl	curl	scuttle
dart	hide	shelter
flutter	jump	wriggle

Plants
They
them g
need p

shoot

roots

Parts

flower

leaf

stalk

Days of the week

Monday

Tuesday

Wednesday

Thursday

Friday

Saturday

Sunday

On Monday we flew to the country. Then we drove to a campsite and set up our tent. On Tuesday morning we searched for buried treasure.

Months of the year

January	July
February	August
March	September
April	October
May	November
June	December

birthday cake

calendar

My birthday is on 20th May.

Times of day

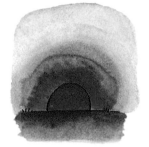

dawn
daybreak

morning

midday

afternoon

dusk
sunset

night

moon

stars

midnight

Telling the time

01:00   one o'clock

02:00   two o'clock

03:00   three o'clock

04:00   four o'clock

05:00   five o'clock

06:00   six o'clock

07:00   seven o'clock

08:00   eight o'clock

09:00   nine o'clock

10:00   ten o'clock

11:00   eleven o'clock

12:00   twelve o'clock

useful words

first	yesterday	after
next	today	eventually
then	tomorrow	last
later	before	finally

59

Opposites

cold

hot

Winter weather can be cold and snowy.

In summer the weather can be hot and sunny.

fast

slow

short

tall

happy

sad

young

old

clean

dirty

up

down

shout

whisper

catch

throw

above

top

below

bottom

old

new

timid

brave

empty

full

high

low

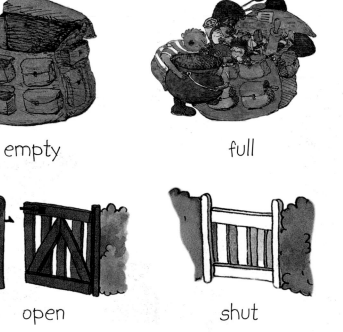

open

shut

asleep

awake

small

big

messy

tidy

Index